D1271155

WITHDRAWN
FROM THE RECORDS OF THE
MID-CONTINENT PUBLIC LIBRARY

JE
Nash, Margaret.
Sammy's secret

MID-CONTINENT PUBLIC LIBRARY
South Independence Branch
13700 E. 35th Street
Independence, MO 64055

SI

Sammy's
Secret

Crabtree Publishing Company
www.crabtreebooks.com

PMB16A, 350 Fifth Avenue
Suite 3308,
New York, NY

616 Welland Avenue
St. Catharines, ON
L2M 5V6

Published by Crabtree Publishing in 2008

First published in 2006 by
Franklin Watts
(A division of Hachette Children's Books)
338 Euston Road
London   NW1 3BH

Text © Margaret Nash 2006
Illustration © Anni Axworthy 2006

The rights of the author and the illustrator of this Work
have been asserted.

All rights reserved. No part of this publication may be
reproduced, stored in a retrieval system, or transmitted
in any form or by any means, electronic, mechanical,
photocopy, recording or otherwise, without the prior
written permission of the copyright owner.

Cataloging-in-Publication data is available at the Library of Congress.

ISBN 978-0-7787-3863-3 (rlb)
ISBN 978-0-7787-3894-7 (pbk)

Series Editor: Jackie Hamley
Series Advisor: Dr Hilary Minns
Series Designer: Peter Scoulding

Printed in the U.S.A.

Sammy's Secret

by Margaret Nash

Illustrated by Anni Axworthy

Crabtree Publishing Company

www.crabtreebooks.com

MID-CONTINENT PUBLIC LIBRARY
South Independence Branch
13700 E. 35th Street
Independence, MO 64055 **SI**

MID-CONTINENT PUBLIC LIBRARY - BTM

3 0003 00722123 5

Margaret Nash

"I think all
cats have secrets.
I'm sure my
cat Tabitha has.
But I know she hasn't
got one like Sammy's!"

Anni Axworthy

"My two dogs
were very unhappy
about me painting
all these cats,
but I had a
good time!"

Sammy couldn't run as fast as Rocky.

Sammy couldn't jump
as high as Jess.

Sammy couldn't climb
as far as Kitty.

9

"You're too small," they said.

Rocky

"You need to grow!"

So Sammy hung
from the door.

13

14

He stretched out
on the floor.

He rolled up in a ball.

But he was still small.

"There is something
I *can* do," said Sammy.

SAMMY

JESS

ROCKY

KITTY

19

And one day, when
the rain beat down ...

... he did it!

Meow! Meow!

23

Notes for adults

TADPOLES are structured to provide support for early readers. The stories may also be used by adults for sharing with young children.

Starting to read alone can be daunting. **TADPOLES** help by providing visual support and repeating high frequency words and phrases. These books will both develop confidence and encourage reading and rereading for pleasure.

If you are reading this book with a child, here are a few suggestions:

1. Make reading fun! Choose a time to read when you and the child are relaxed and have time to share the story.
2. Talk about the story before you start reading. Look at the cover and the blurb. What might the story be about? Why might the child like it?
3. Encourage the child to reread the story, and to retell the story in their own words, using the illustrations to remind them what has happened.
4. Discuss the story and see if the child can relate it to their own experiences, or perhaps compare it to another story they know.
5. Give praise! Children learn best in a positive environment.

If you enjoyed this book, why not try another TADPOLES story?

At the End of the Garden
9780778738503 RLB
9780778738817 PB

Bad Luck, Lucy!
9780778738510 RLB
9780778738824 PB

Ben and the Big Balloon
9780778738602 RLB
9780778738916 PB

Crabby Gabby
9780778738527 RLB
9780778738831 PB

Five Teddy Bears
9780778738534 RLB
9780778738848 PB

I'm Taller Than You!
9780778738541 RLB
9780778738855 PB

Leo's New Pet
9780778738558 RLB
9780778738862 PB

Little Troll
9780778738565 RLB
9780778738879 PB

Mop Top
9780778738572 RLB
9780778738886 PB

My Auntie Susan
9780778738589 RLB
9780778738893 PB

My Big, New Bed
9780778738596 RLB
9780778738909 PB

Pirate Pete
9780778738619 RLB
9780778738923 PB

Runny Honey
9780778738626 RLB
9780778738930 PB

Sammy's Secret
9780778738633 RLB
9780778738947 PB

Sam's Sunflower
9780778738640 RLB
9780778738954 PB